Addict 2.0
Andre's Story

By Porsha Deun

Books by Porsha Deun

<u>The Love Lost Series</u>
Love Lost
Love Lost Forever
Love Lost Revenge

<u>The Addict Series</u>
Addict – A Fatal Attraction Story
Addict 2.0 – Andre's Story
Addict 3.0 – DeAngelo's Story (July2021)
Addict – DeMario's Story (Aug 2021)

<u>Standalones</u>
Intoxic (Oct 2021)

<u>Children's Book</u>
Princesses Can Do Anything! (June 2021)

ADDICT 2.0 – ANDRE'S STORY. Copyright © 2021 by Porsha Deun. All rights reserved. Published in Grand Blanc, MI. Printed in the United States of America for Porsha Deun, LLC. For information, email Porsha Deun, porshadeun@gmail.com.

All characters, places, and events are fiction and not real. Any likeness is a coincidence and not intentional.

All rights reserved. No parts of this book may be reproduced by any mechanical, photographic, or electronic process, or in the form of a phonographic recording; nor may it be stored in a retrieval system, transmitted, or otherwise copied for public or private use – other than for "fair use" as brief quotations embodied in articles and reviews – without prior written permission of the author.

ISBN (paperback): 978-1-7364778-8-5

Library of Congress Control Number: Pending

To my best friend Daphne,

My Covid Survivor. You are truly one of my soulmates. Thank you for being your crazy, loving self.

Addict 2.0
Andre's Story

Porsha Deun

Chapter 1

The quarter was always a good place to go hunting for some ladies. Between the NOLA natives and the constant flow of tourists, there was always something new. Always something ready and willing.

Drinks in the quarter were cheaper than anywhere else in the city. So, you can treat a lady, especially an out-of-town lady, for cheap and she would be none-the-wiser.

I stopped in Bar Tonique and ordered a Vesper at the bar. I scanned the tavern for something appealing. Though there were plenty of ladies in there, some of them checking me out, none of them were my fancy.

I liked my women thick, with real curves. I was a proud BBW lover. Black BBWs at that. Wasn't nothing like the pussy of a Black Big Beautiful Woman. So soft, wet, gushy and warm. They would beg for a big dick like mine to sink all the way in. They're titties were the best too. Just the thought of a big pair of natural titties bouncing while I'm in a tight fat pussy made me begin to harden.

After finishing my drink, I decided there wasn't anything for me in this spot, so I left. Lafitte's Blacksmith Shop Bar was my next stop for a Hurricane. I walked around sipping on my strong mixed drink with my button-down shirt open, black jeans, and matte black loafers. After about five minutes was when I spotted

ADDICT 2.0 – ANDRE'S STORY

her, the woman who would turn my world upside down and I would later give up everything for.

I didn't know that at the time though.

I stood against the brick of a building watching her from across the street. Tall, thick wide hips, big titties. Beautiful face. Confident. She walked like she owed the world nothing, but the world owed her a big kiss on her ass.

Oh, I wanted to kiss and lick that ass and more.

I followed her until she went into the Curio. It looked like she was alone, but she could've been meeting someone. Inside the little European bar, I stood behind her. Her perfume was as intoxicating as the Hurricane I chugged down while I followed her.

"How many?" the hostess asked her.

"One."

"Make that two," I said. The beautiful BBW in front of me turned around and looked me up and down. "That's if it is okay with you," I added.

She bit her bottom lip. "Yeah, I'm good with that."

"Andre," I said as I put my hand out for hers.

"Destiny."

She put her hand in mine and I kissed her knuckles before looking at the hostess and confirming that it would be two of us for dinner. Sexy Miss Destiny and I followed the hostess holding hands like we're familiar lovers. I pulled her chair out for her, then took my seat.

Damn, she was fine. Her dark skin was smooth and glowed, and her bright pink top complimented her complexion perfectly. "What brings you to the quarter?" she asked me.

"I was looking for you."

"You say that to all the ladies, I bet."

"I do. It works. This time I mean it." I was surprised by how much I did. That was how I knew she was different; unlike any woman I had ever interacted with. I was hers from the moment I laid eyes on her and didn't know it.

"You say that to all the ladies, too?"

"No."

She gave me a smirk that was both wicked and sexy. Her accent told me she was a local. That's good because I was already thinking I was going to want to have her more than once.

"What would you like to drink?" a waitress asked us.

"Sparkly Rosè for me," Destiny said.

"I'll have an Abita Amber," I answered. The waitress walked away. Destiny and I never took our eyes off each other. "What brings you to the quarter?" I asked her in return.

"Looking to satisfy a hunger or two."

"Single?"

"You wouldn't be sitting here with me if I wasn't." The waitress brought our drinks and we both took a sip.

"Have you had a chance to look at the menu?"

"Not yet," I said. Still, I kept my eyes on Destiny.

"I'll give you a few more minutes." Then she was off again.

"What are you hungry for, Miss Destiny?" Something about my question got to her in a good way. She gasped and bit her plump bottom lip. My eyes traveled from her lips, down her neck, and rested on the swell of her breasts. *Yeah, I definitely wanted to see my dick poke through the top of her breasts as she held them together while I fucked her titties.*

"Several things, food being the least of them now."

"In that case, what do you say about us getting out of here and going dancing? See where the evening takes us."

Her smile widened. Beautiful pearly white teeth with her dark skin...whew. I found myself wondering what more I could do to keep her smiling at me like that. "I'd like that a lot."

I pulled out my wallet, tossed $40 on the table, and put my hand out for hers.

There was always a party on the streets of the Quarter. It wasn't long before we found ourselves in the middle of one and were dancing to the music.

ADDICT 2.0 – ANDRE'S STORY

You know that song by Next that's about a woman dancing on a man so close that she turned him on, and his dick got hard? Yeah, that was me in that moment with Destiny. I knew she could feel me, and she seemed to be loving it.

She kept grinding and shaking her big round ass on me. I wasn't sure if she was doing it for me, the other people looking, or both. I didn't care. All I knew was that she wanted me just as much as I wanted her.

The humid air seemed to be electric, adding to the intensity of the heat between us. Sweat beaded on her back in the places where her skin was exposed. I wanted to mix her sweat with mine from my chest and abs.

I squeezed her hips and pulled her even more into me, controlling her pace. Really, I was making sure I was keeping up with her and that the seductive shakes of her ass didn't bounce me off and away from her. *Baby girl could move.*

That was one of the things I liked the most about local girls over the tourists, especially the women who lived north and east of the transcontinental railroad. Local girls, southern girls in general, could shake their asses like no other. Northern girls were alright at it. Island girls could wind their hips like crazy. Still, I would take me a fluffy southern Black Queen before any others.

My lucky hands were gripping the hips of such a Queen right then.

Chapter 2

I bent down over Destiny, who was laying on her back on the edge of the hotel room bed with her legs back and wide. I'd been driving my dick into her almost from the moment we got into the hotel room about thirty minutes ago.

"Wrap your arms around my neck," I told her as I tucked my hands under her hips and ass. Once she did, I lifted her up.

"Woah, shit," she said as I picked her up. She wasn't expecting me to do that.

"I got you, baby."

"You sure?"

I looked her right in her eyes. "My baby, I got you."

Something registered in her eyes. Something that let me know she knew I meant beyond just that night. I usually never want any woman more than once, but from the moment I saw Destiny, I knew this was going to be different.

With my arms under her thighs and my hands gripping her ass, I worked her bottom back and forth on my dick. Destiny moaned like she was possessed. I've never met anyone so uninhibited in their sexual desires before. Most women I picked up were guarded, unwilling to let go in order to achieve new sexual heights.

Destiny was fully in tune with herself and I wanted to be in tune with her. Even with the air on, we were still sweating from the heat we created. My hands kept sliding off her ass, making it

ADDICT 2.0 – ANDRE'S STORY

impossible for me to grip her and keep going like we were. I walked over to a wall and pinned her against it. With her firmly in place, I stroked her deep and long.

Destiny's nails dug into my back. I was happy she had fake nails on, so it didn't hurt as much and wouldn't take skin off like real nails did. Her moans were so loud that whoever was in the room next to ours started banging on the wall as a way to tell us to keep it down. Destiny started to yell back at them, but I put my lips on hers, quieting her fussing and moans at the same time while keeping her in the moment, keeping her mentally with me just as she was physically. I felt the tension in her body from being irritated by our temporary neighbors leave her body as I continued to kiss and stroke her.

Her pussy was so tight and wet. I loved how her body responded to my touch. I could feel myself getting ready to cum. I hoped she didn't mind going multiple rounds because I wasn't done with her yet. "Where do you want me to cum?" I panted between thrusts.

"I want to taste you," she said in a rushed moan.

I gave her a few more strokes before releasing her legs from over my arms and told her to get on her knees. Destiny slid down between my body and the wall. She took me into her mouth and moved my hand out the way so she could work me over. I blasted off in an instant.

With my head back and eyes closed tight, my semen shot into her mouth, and it was a big load. *What did she do to me? Wait, did she swallow? I think she swallowed.*

I open my eyes and look down on the plush beauty still working me, keeping me hard after I nutted. She must had known I was watching because she moved to the base of my dick, just above my balls, looked me in my eyes and slowly dragged her tongue to the top of the head before swirling it around without breaking eye contact.

She definitely swallowed.

Porsha Deun

"You are going to make me fall in love with you if you keep sucking me like that."

"Fall in lust with me. Don't fall in love."

I thought that was a strange thing for her to say, because who doesn't want to fall in love at some point. I shrugged it off as her not wanting to rush things since we only just met. In time, we would both be falling for each other I thought.

"I'm already in lust with you," I said because I felt like I had to say something after her comment. It wouldn't be until much later when I realized how much she meant what she said and by then, it was much too late for me.

ADDICT 2.0 – ANDRE'S STORY

Chapter 3

It had been a few months since me and Destiny met in the Quarter. To say that she had a high sex drive was an understatement. I've never met a woman who thought about sex like a man.

Which was both a joy and hell.

I caught feelings for Destiny, and she had been entertaining some other dude for a month now while still fucking me. Even though I wasn't with her any less than I was before this other dude came along, if I wanted more of her time and attention, I wouldn't have been able to get it.

I *wanted* more of her time and attention.

Even as we laid in her bed after going a couple of rounds, I didn't want to think about another guy being here with her. Not on no shit like I wished she was a virgin when I met her type of stuff, because no virgin would have hooked me with their sex game the way Destiny did. I didn't want another woman and I didn't want her to have anyone else either.

I wanted to ask…no, demand more of her. I wanted to be her man. Her one and only man. I didn't know how to approach the topic with her, especially knowing she viewed relationships as limiting. I struggled with how I could make her see that I could give her everything she could possibly need and more if she'd be willing to give me a chance.

I wanted to see her happy and I badly wanted that happiness to include me. That's the only reason why I was still

ADDICT 2.0 – ANDRE'S STORY

around at that point and not fucking anyone else. I would have done whatever she asked of me in order to stay in her world.

Destiny said something to me that I missed, being lost in my thoughts as I was.

"What'd you say, my baby?"

"Have you ever had a threesome?" she repeated.

"I've had a couple. What, you got a girl in mind that you want to share?"

"Not exactly."

Quiet settled between us as she left me to ponder on her meaning. As the answer came to me, my body tensed. "Aye, I'm not with no gay shit, Destiny. I like pussy. *Your pussy*," I said as I cupped her fat box with my hand.

"You don't have to be. DeAngelo isn't either. You two would be fucking me, not each other."

"You've already talked to him about it, I take it." This was taking sharing her to a whole new level and I already didn't like the level we were on at the time.

"I knew you would need more convincing," she said as she nodded. Destiny turned over to her side to face me.

My breath deepened as I fought with the thought of this unfamiliar territory. Here I was wrecking my mind on how to convince Destiny to be mine and she was trying to convince me to fuck her while this…DeAngelo, fucks her too!

What if this is what she needed to stay happy?

"Please, Andre," she begged between kisses on my stomach that headed south. "If it goes well, we can do it once a week like that."

I knew by 'we' she meant the three of us. Closing my eyes, I draped an arm over my eyes as Destiny took my dick into her mouth. I was well aware of what she was doing. Nonetheless, I could do nothing to stop it. I was going to give into her no matter how much I didn't want to. No matter how much I hated the idea of sharing her in any way.

With her head bobbing over my groin, my mind raced with all the ways this could go wrong. Clearly, she liked his sex game well enough that she kept seeing him. All kinds of things started going through my head. *What if she ended up liking sex with him more than sex with me, especially since he seems to be down with whatever she came up with? What if he is down with it because he's in love with her too?*

In my mind, this had to be it. Destiny was beautiful, sexy, confident, and independent. Sex with her was good to boot, too. This was the moment I went from simply giving into Destiny's desires to doing whatever I could do to fight for the woman I wanted. The woman I cared for.

"Yes."

She took a long and hard suck up my dick, coming off of it with a pop. "What was that?" she asked with a smack of her lips.

"I'll do it, if this is what you really want."

A wide grin came across her face. Just like the one at the restaurant the night we met. "It's what I want."

"Then I'm yours, however you want me."

Her smile turned salacious before she went down on me again. Destiny's head game had always been fire, but what she was doing to me after getting her way was like she was trying to make love to my dick. Giving me all her love and appreciation for giving her what she wanted with her mouth work. It wasn't long until all thoughts of what I agreed to do went away long enough for me to get lost and erupt in her mouth.

ADDICT 2.0 – ANDRE'S STORY

Chapter 4

Not even gonna lie, I was nervous as shit sitting in the living room of Destiny's condo, despite having been over there countless times since we met months ago. She got me and DeAngelo sitting down here waiting on her. *Did she not know that getting over here to do this was a lot for me?*

I was glad I did several rounds of pushups to help calm my nerves some before leaving my place. Not only did it help with some of the nervous energy I was feeling, but my muscles looked more pumped up in the moment. I was also glad that me and this dude look nothing alike.

DeAngelo was slimmer than me, still cut, but slender compared to my thick muscular frame. Dark skinned with a low fade. Knowing how much Destiny liked pulling on my hair while we were going at it, I was glad she couldn't do that with him too.

"How long you been knowing Destiny?" he asked me.

"A few months," I said. I didn't know if that was a sign that they didn't really talk and hadn't tried to get to know each other or if he was just trying to break the tension in the room. He nodded at my answer. I didn't bother asking him the same because I already knew and didn't care. I had known Destiny longer. I would continue to know her after he was gone, of that I was sure.

DeAngelo nodded again, seeming to recognize my stance. "Why'd you agree to do this?"

I didn't answer him. Instead, I stared at him. He thought he was so perceptive, so I decided to let him figure it out.

ADDICT 2.0 – ANDRE'S STORY

DeAngelo dropped his head and chuckled before looking back up to me. "Oh, shit. You're in love with her! Does she know?" he asked while pointing to the ceiling.

I tilted my head to the side.

"Either you haven't made it clear to her or she knows and doesn't care as long as you are along for the ride."

"Whatever makes her happy," I said as a simple explanation. I hadn't told Destiny about my feelings for her, but eventually she will see and return my affections. There was no way she wouldn't, in my mind.

"You know what she does for a living, right?"

I nodded. I was well aware that Destiny paid her bills with money she made from her private clients as a Dominatrix. Clients she whipped, spanked, and demeaned.

"Hoes like that—"

"Don't ever refer to Destiny as that," I snapped. We had a stare off that lasted a few moments before DeAngelo shrugged and put his hands up. The tension between us was thick and the quiet was even heavier. That was until DeAngelo spoke again.

"Can I give you a piece of advice, man to man?"

I couldn't believe he thought I would take any of his advice seriously. I nodded anyway, curious as to what he had to say.

"Protect yourself. Don't get wrapped up into more of Destiny's shit than you already have. If you don't, you *will* get hurt."

I adjusted in my seat as a way of shrugging him off. What did he know? He wouldn't...couldn't understand. He didn't know Destiny like I did. She was worthy of love and I was going to be the one to give it to her.

"Whatever," DeAngelo said when he realized I was dismissing his so-called advice. "I've met her type a few times before. Don't say you weren't warned." He changed his attention. "Hey, Destiny!" he yelled. "How long you gonna have us waiting down here?"

"Not any longer," she said as she rounded the corner from her foyer coming into the living room. Destiny was completely naked, body oiled up to make her curves dangerous and dark skin look all the more edible. Her hair was in a new style from the last time I saw her just a couple of days ago. Instead of the big wild afro I was used to, her hair was in long braids that fell past her waist. The braids made her look more regal, more queen-like than usual.

Her beauty always took my breath away. "Destiny," I whispered as I stood to greet her.

She came over to me and started undoing my pants. I caressed her cheek, and she gave me a small smile. I loved all her smiles and would take any she offered me. She worked my pants down and off my legs as she went down to her knees. I sat down on the couch. As her mouth enclosed around my dick, I let my head relax back to the top of the couch as I silently celebrated the fact that she came to me first.

ADDICT 2.0 – ANDRE'S STORY

Chapter 5

I was lost in the warmth, wetness, and tight suction of Destiny's mouth when I notice a change in how she was moving. I opened my eyes and saw DeAngelo had made his way behind and inside of her. Destiny moaned and it brought out a jealousness in me I had never felt before.

I didn't want to hear her moans of pleasure from what DeAngelo was doing to her. My hands went to her hair, tangling into her new braids before I pulled her head down further on my dick until I was well into her throat. Silence, outside of the sound of his body smacking into hers.

Though I was fighting the skin slapping against skin sounds, I couldn't help but love the bounce it was giving Destiny's head with my dick down her throat. She tapped my leg to let me know she needed air. She was gasping as soon as I let her up, but I never took my hands out of her hair. As soon as she started to moan again, I pulled her head back down.

"You ready to get in here?" DeAngelo asked me.

I took it as an insult. Like he thought he needed to give me permission to get something I had been getting much longer than he had. In response, I pulled Destiny's head up high enough to make her back straighten, bent down to pick her up, effectively taking her from DeAngelo. For a second, I thought about having her ride me, but I changed my mind. I needed to remind Destiny of what we had, what I brought to the table.

ADDICT 2.0 – ANDRE'S STORY

Rotating us while I had her hovering over my lap, I laid her down on her back on the couch and slid between her legs before she had time to adjust. I heard DeAngelo give a sarcastic laugh.

Yeah, fuck you too.

Destiny moaned as I dug hard and deep into her. These were the moans I wanted to hear. The moans that meant something, everything, to me. I kept my face positioned to the side of Destiny's to block DeAngelo from not only seeing hers, but from coming up to get some head while I was inside of her.

"Fuck, Andre!" Destiny sung.

"This is what you want, my baby?"

"Yes. Fuck, yes!" My teeth dragged along the soft skin of her neck as her nails dug into my back. "Anndrrreee…" she sung my name and I could feel her walls and legs shaking.

My name was called first.

I made her cum first.

She came to me first.

These thoughts along with Destiny's orgasmic quaking drove me even harder. I wanted to erase traces and memories of any and everyone. A possessive feeling came over me that I couldn't control. It was like I was overcome by something else. Something I would later call love.

My hands found their way around her neck. I dug into her pussy deeper and harder like my dick was trying to communicate with her heart and soul through Morris code. Our eyes locked on each other's. Destiny looked like she was lost in ecstasy and scared at the same time. My nut was right there on the edge but refused to take the leap. I pounded into her, desperate for release and she scratched my arms in desperation for air. I loosened my grip on her neck, allowing her to breathe. She frantically pulled in lung-fulls of air as I tried to push my orgasm forward.

"Don't stop, Andre. Don't. Fucking. Stop." I had no intention of stopping before my kids roamed freely in her pussy. "Choke me again."

My response was silent but complicit. There was a slight grin on her face. It was beautiful and sexy as fuck. Her smile began to break down a part of the invisible barrier that kept my nut back.

Destiny squeezed her walls tight. I didn't know if it was intentional or not. *Bullshit. It was definitely intentional.* She owned every part of me, including my nut. I realized then that I couldn't cum because she didn't want me to.

"Fuck, Destiny!" I growled. She released her grip on my dick and tightened right back up. The barrier cracked some more as I continued stroking her with fervor, racing to fly over that cliff.

Destiny released and squeezed again.

The barrier shattered. My cum released inside Destiny with a growl that came up from deep within my chest. My dick was throbbing so hard that it hurt. Destiny was having an orgasm of her own which was prolonging mine.

I turned her neck loose as I came down and collapsed on top of her as we both caught our breaths.

Destiny kissed my shoulder. "That was amazing," she whispered.

I kissed her neck. "Yeah, it was." We giggled and it was bliss. Bliss that was taken away too soon.

"There's another dick waiting over here for you, Destiny," DeAngelo said. "Or do you not know how threesomes are supposed to work?"

My body stiffened. For a second, I forgot he was there. Destiny did too and told him so. Destiny wiggled to get me to let her up but instead I tighten my grip around her body.

"You agreed to this, remember," Destiny whispered to me.

That doesn't mean I have to like it.

ADDICT 2.0 – ANDRE'S STORY

Instead of voicing my thoughts, I sighed and slowly lifted off her until I was sitting up on the couch. I wanted to punch him for every step she took towards him. Just because he was there. Just because he existed.

Destiny started sucking his dick and I sat across the room from them, watching her get pleasure from pleasing another man while I worked my dick back to life. I wasn't about to let him have her to himself the way I just did.

One thing that always got me hard was going down on Destiny. I decided that was what I was going to do. As she sucked him, I laid on my back on the floor under her and ate her. I've never eaten a woman after shooting her club up. This seemed like a good enough reason to start doing it now. Destiny moaned as she rode my face, her songs of pleasure drowning out the sounds of dick sucking.

I made her cum like that and was intending on doing it again until DeAngelo ruined that idea. "Turn around so I can get up in that pussy," he told her.

I hated the way he talked to her, like she was nothing more than a sex toy or a piece of flesh. Destiny did as he said, was on all fours on the floor while DeAngelo pushed the chaise out the way to make room for himself. Destiny sucked me and I did the same thing I did earlier to quiet her moans.

After a while, I needed to be inside Destiny again. The head was good, but I wanted to cum inside her again. Not giving a damn about this other dude and what he was trying to do, I pulled Destiny up to straddle and ride me.

"Now y'all are figuring this shit out," DeAngelo says. I didn't get what he meant by it until Destiny stiffened. He smacked her ass hard. "Relax, damn. Don't act like you ain't had it like this before."

Destiny's done anal with him before? Her and I had never gone there. Was that why she felt it necessary to seek out someone else?

Porsha Deun

I made a mental note to give Destiny anal regularly when we were together. I couldn't have another guy giving Destiny something I wasn't. I could never win her over like that.

She started moving once she was comfortable, but her grinds weren't enough. This three-way positioning didn't allow me to get as deep in her as I wanted to be when she normally rode me. I thrusted upwards to meet and match Destiny, getting exactly where I wanted to be inside of her.

It wasn't long before the three of us were all moving together. I sucked on her big, beautiful breasts as they hung in my face while I held onto her waist. The harder DeAngelo thrusted, the harder I did too. He wasn't going to outdo me or out pleasure me where Destiny was concerned. Not any longer, that was.

Her moans were wild and sexy as hell. That and learning what I needed to be doing more of were the only things I was grateful for this threesome for. A familiar shake went through Destiny's legs and it was right on time, because I was ready to pop off too. Her and I orgasmed together moaning and growling. Shortly after, DeAngelo had her on her knees in front of him as he squirted his jizz all over her face.

She's not your personal porn star you fucking bastard.

ADDICT 2.0 – ANDRE'S STORY

Chapter 6

"Are you serious?"

"You got used to DeAngelo being around. You'll get used to DeMario, too."

I all but rolled my eyes and looked away from her. *'Used to'* wasn't exactly the phrase I would have used. More like, I begrudgingly did it because I was in love. I only kept doing it because the threesomes seemed to make Destiny happy.

"Come on Dre. It will be fun."

"Fun for *you*. You don't have to…" I stopped because the one thing I feared most was driving her away by expressing my feelings knowing she wasn't in a place to hear or accept them yet. "Were you not satisfied when it was just you and me?"

"Yes and no."

The *'yes'* elated my soul. The immediate *'no'* that came after was crushing. It must had shown on my face because Destiny went on to explain.

"Sex with you is great, Andre. Mind blowing. I've had some of the best sex of my life with you. Me wanting DeAngelo and DeMario has nothing to do with you. You aren't lacking in any way, trust me. It's just that…one dick can't do to me what three dicks can at the same time. It's nothing personal, so don't take it that way."

"That's easier said than done."

"Andre." Destiny climbed into the bed and sat close to me. "Andre. You were the first member of my…magic dick team,

ADDICT 2.0 – ANDRE'S STORY

if you will. You are a part of the magic that brings me so much joy. That magic is almost perfect, can be perfect, if you agree."

"What would happen if I didn't?" Destiny pulled away from me as her back went erect and her face bunched up like what I said was the most unexpected thing ever to her. "I don't like sharing you like this," I added.

"Technically, I'm not yours to share or not share, Andre."

Those words stung even though I knew it was true. She had no idea how much I wanted it to not be true. Monogamy wasn't either of our thing when we met, which only added to my attraction to her, but now, in the moment, I was at a loss. I knew I risked losing her if I kept pushing. I closed my eyes at the thought because it brought me pain greater than watching her enjoy someone else.

I am a part of the magic that brings her so much joy. I am a part of the magic that brings her so much joy.

I fell back onto the bed in frustration as I chanted this in my head and stared at the ceiling. I didn't want to do this, but I had to. I couldn't lose her. I wouldn't have been able to make Destiny one day see that I loved her if I wasn't around to show her.

"Destiny, you are killing me," I said without looking at her.

"Is that a yes?"

I released a heavy sigh. "Yes."

"Then death will be enjoyable for you," she said as she laid her body over mine. She kissed my lips. "If it is any consolation prize, of the three of y'all, you are the only one I kiss."

"I bet you say that to the others," I said, throwing her words to me the night we met back at her.

"I don't. I don't have to because I don't kiss them. *You* are the only one I kiss."

With that piece of information, I put my fingers in her hair and pulled her face down to mine. My kiss was soft, full of my affection and love for her, but it was also possessive. Destiny was a physical woman. The only way I could communicate my feelings for her in a way that wouldn't scare her off was to do it physically. She wasn't ready for words yet.

So, I did just that. With one arm wrapped around her luscious body, I turned us over so that I was on top of her. Destiny gave me a soft sensual moan as I poured more of my love for her into our kiss and she wrapped her legs around my waist. She was still wet from our earlier session, which allowed me to slide into her with ease.

My strokes were slow and strong. I told her how much I loved and wanted her with every stroke. Between my feelings for her and the anger and jealousy I felt in having to share her with yet another, my body was physically trembling while I made love to the woman who was more than willing to drive me to madness.

Destiny moaned my name and asked me to speed up. I couldn't. I wouldn't. Speeding up would have taken away the meaning of it. This wasn't just a mere fuck this time. Instead, I made my thrusts more forceful. Gave more punctuation and emphasis to every stroke of love, admiration, and silent promises of forever.

This was enough to satisfy Destiny as she stopped asking me to go faster. As I got lost in her, I hoped she would get lost in me, too. With my body, I told her everything I couldn't say to her with words yet. Destiny moaned and swore. Her body tensed in ways I had not felt her do before, like she was trying to fight something off. *Her emotions, maybe?*

I pressed my lips to hers to distract her enough from her internal fight that she gave into those feelings, letting them rise to the surface and meeting me there. My tongue plunged deep into her mouth, over taking her. With every caress of my tongue against hers, I urge her to see me and love me back. *All I wanted is for her to love me back.*

Her body relaxed and tensed again and again. She was fighting hard with herself. Between kisses, I whispered to her. "Let go."

ADDICT 2.0 – ANDRE'S STORY

It took her a few moments, but she replied with a whisper. "No."

A few moments later, I said it again. This time, I didn't wait for or let her reply. I plunged my tongue and dick into her deep at the same time. She relaxed again and I kept kissing her to keep her that way. Destiny moaned into my mouth and I into hers. We stayed in our slow, powerful, and emotionally charged sexing until we peaked together. Destiny held me tighter with her arms and legs while she convulsed around me and I poured into her. This was our first time cumming together and it was everything I ever hoped it would be. I kissed her neck and shoulders, continued to shower her with love and affection that I couldn't express any other way.

"Let me up," Destiny said with a pat on my back once she was able to catch her breath.

I rolled off her and onto my side. The temperature of the room dropped. The emotional charge in the air around us turned dark and broken. I called after her as she hurried out of the bed and into her bathroom, but she never responded or looked back towards me.

I fell back onto the bed kicking myself. *That was too much for her. I risked losing her by expressing my feelings when she wasn't ready to even acknowledge them in any way. What was I going to do if she decides to end things with me?*

In slow movements, I got out the bed and walked over to the door of her en-suite. I feared I fucked up in a big way. I listened closely and there was nothing. No sound came from the other side of the door. I knocked on it. "Destiny."

A couple of moments pass and still nothing. "Destiny," I said a little more panicked.

"I think you should go, Andre."

Go. No. No. No. I can't leave her like this. She can't leave me or order me out of her life.

Porsha Deun

My mind started racing with things to say or do to fight for her, to keep her in my life. There was only one word I could come up with. "No!"

"I don't mean for good, Andre. I'm not ending this. For today…for now… go. We both need time to get ourselves together, to remember what this is and isn't."

What this is and isn't?

Those last five words were a dagger into my soul. "Destiny…I…" I closed my eyes tight as if that would somehow block or end the pain I felt.

"I'm not ending this," she repeated as if she knew the ending of her last statement did not register to me. "I need you. I just need the rest of today by myself."

"Can I see you before I go?" If I could see her, I could comfort her somehow, put her at ease.

Silence was all I got. It was gut wrenching.

I walked back to where my clothes were near the bed, picked them up and put them on. I had never felt so defeated in my life. All I wanted to do was tell her how I felt, and I managed to fuck that up, pushed her away from me instead of bringing her closer. *What could I do now but give her the space she asked for? I hadn't left yet, but I already missed her.*

I stopped in front of the bathroom door before leaving and it opened. Destiny stood in the doorframe with a satin robe on. She gave me a small smile before telling me that we were good. I started to apologize but she stopped me. "We're good. Good pussy swear."

We both chuckled.

"Good pussy swear? Like a pinky swear?" I asked. That was new. Destiny nodded. "Can I call to check on you later?" She nodded again. I wanted to kiss her before I left, but I feared doing so would have set us back even more. "Later, beautiful."

"Later."

I left her place happy I hadn't lost her but hurt that my feelings were not received well.

ADDICT 2.0 – ANDRE'S STORY

AFTER DESTINY COMMITS MURDER

ADDICT 2.0 – ANDRE'S STORY

Chapter 7

I sat in the courtroom and listened as the A.D.A. presented their case. I was there every day. Listened as DeAngelo testified against Destiny. I always knew she meant nothing to him. I understood that DeMario was his brother, but for him to turn on Destiny the way he did showed how much he was not worthy of her or in any way faithful to her. Not like I was. I never lied to or used Destiny the way those twins did. DeMario deserved whatever he had coming to him for disrespecting her like that. He shouldn't have never got involved with Destiny, *my Destiny*, when he had a girlfriend.

They only saw her for the sex. They didn't see her for the queen she was and will always be.

I sat there and listened after DeMario's former girlfriend made Destiny sound like a manipulative psychopath. They didn't understand her. Destiny didn't like change she wasn't in control of. DeMario lied to her. Hurt her. If he hadn't did what he did, none of us would be here right now. In fact, if DeAngelo never came along, none of this would have happened and my Destiny would have been where she should have been, with me. This was their doing.

Sitting in the courtroom watching them escort her away during the trial and at her sentencing was hard, but I was still there. I would always be there for Destiny. I told her that every day before she left the courtroom with her assigned guards.

ADDICT 2.0 – ANDRE'S STORY

Me and DeAngelo got into a fight outside the courthouse one day. He couldn't understand how I could standby Destiny and I told him that this was all his brother's fault. He didn't want to hear it, but it was the truth. The Asian girlfriend got in the middle of us and broke it up.

Today was my first day to visit Destiny in prison. I wrote her every day and asked that she add me to her visitor's list in each one until she agreed to. I haven't seen my beautiful Destiny in over a month and haven't had her in even longer.

Destiny walked in and my heart started pounding hard. She made the horrible orange jumpsuit look halfway decent. I stood and waited for her to make it to the table I picked out for us in the visiting lounge. I gave her a hug and gave her the flowers I brought with me.

"Hey beautiful."

"Hey, Andre."

"How are you holding up in here? Are you being treated fair?"

"Slow down," she said with a sigh. "Things are okay, considering."

I looked into her eyes waiting for her to give me more, but she didn't. "Any chance of your attorney fighting for you to possibly get parole later?"

"There is no parole for first degree murder in the state of Louisiana," Destiny said flatly.

I knew that but I was hoping. "Well, regardless of how long you are here or where you are, I'm still here for you. I will come see you as much as I can."

"Why?" She looked at me with eyes that were confused yet cold.

"What?" Destiny had to know by now how I felt about her. I was there for her in court, after all.

"Andre, I'm in here for the rest of my life. There is no chance for anything with anyone outside these walls. Why are you sticking around me when we were just fucking?"

"It was never just sex for me. You know that. I told you that."

Destiny sighed. "I don't deserve you."

"No, don't say that. The other ones didn't deserve you. You wouldn't be here if it wasn't for them."

"You really believe that, don't you?" Destiny asked.

"It's true."

"We're a match made in delusional heaven."

I frowned at her, not getting what she meant. "I tried to schedule us a conjugal visit but apparently that isn't allowed here."

"It's not allowed in the state, or most of the country for that matter." She looked me up and down. "Is that really why you're here? Hoping you can get some more of this?"

"No. I told you it was more than sex for me, but I don't want anyone else."

"I can't give you what you want no more than you could give me what I wanted alone."

I started to say something but paused as her words registered in my head. "You give me more than you know," I finally said.

"You're obsessed with me. An addict of what you think we had."

"I'm in love with you," I corrected her.

"I told you not to fall in love with me." Destiny gave me a hard look. One that bore through me and made me feel empty. "You shouldn't come back here again."

"What? Destiny, no. I need to be able to see you, be near you."

"Do you know what I've missed about you, Andre?"

I shook my head, but I was happy to hear that she missed me in some fashion.

"Your dick. The way you fucked me. The way you ate my pussy. I used to like the way you went along with whatever I put

ADDICT 2.0 – ANDRE'S STORY

in front of you but now…now it's just pathetic. There is nothing I need or want you for now."

I was stunned. Hurt. Broken. Her words took my breath away and I struggled to catch it as I begun to hyperventilate in front of her. "You don't need me? Or want me?"

"It was the dick for me. Yeah, you look good and all, but it was the dick. I won't be getting *dick* again unless a male guard decides to give me some."

I slammed my fist down on the table, and she jumped. My breath was ragged from the anger, jealousy, and pain that coursed through my veins. Several people looked our way and the guards were now watching us more closely. "Destiny, I love you. I have always loved you. Don't talk about another man touching you! I can't take it. Not another one."

Destiny stared at me as if I said the absolute worst thing possible to her. It didn't help that the words came out rushed with fury. I said it out of frustration, anger, and jealousy. This visit was going all wrong.

"I'm sorry," I said.

She sighed. "Andre, I need you to hear me when I say this. Hear me more than I was willing to hear DeMario when he said he was finished with me." I looked at her with eyes hopeful that she would finally reciprocate the feelings I've felt for her since our first night together. "I do not feel that way towards you. I shut down that part of myself long before I met you."

"But when we lived together—"

"I was acting," Destiny interrupted. "I used you for a little more than your dick then. I had to in order to make it look like I had let go of DeMario before I acted out my revenge."

"You used me?" I was confused. I thought we made so much progress in the weeks we lived together after DeAngelo and DeMario left her. It was finally just the two of us as it was always supposed to be. And she faked it. "My life has been about you from the moment we met."

"The sex was good, beyond good when we met. Maybe I shouldn't have put it on you so good," Destiny said with a dry laugh.

I didn't find the humor in this. "We are supposed to be together," I stated. My words were angry.

"That. Can't. Happen." Destiny's words were sharp, cutting at my soul. "It was never going to happen, even if I hadn't committed murder. There was a time, long before I met you, where that could have been a possibility. I haven't been that person for quite some time. Go home, Andre. Don't come back. Don't write me again. Besides, this visit is upsetting my lover sitting across the room with her family."

I looked around the room until my eyes met those of a brown-eyed woman with a large mess of curls on her head sitting with an older couple. Her parents, maybe. The woman didn't look happy.

"You. Belong. With. Me," I huffed. My anger was boiling to levels no one had ever taken them before.

"Okay, we're done here." Destiny stood and I immediately did the same. I grabbed her face with both hands and kissed her. There was no time to be gentle. I forced my tongue into her mouth to deepen the kiss, desperate to remind her of what we had and could still have. Show her how perfect we were together.

"Hey! That's not allowed!" a guard yelled at us.

I pulled open the top of her jumpsuit to reveal her lose large breasts that were underneath. A guard pulled me off her before I could get a nipple into my mouth or get a good feel of them. I fought against the guard while talking to Destiny who was trying to pull herself back together.

"Don't say we're over! Don't leave me!" I yelled at her as the guards wrestled me out of the visiting room.

At the security desk, I was informed that my visiting privileges were revoked for ninety days. The thought of not being able to see the woman I loved for that long pained me. That...other

ADDICT 2.0 – ANDRE'S STORY

woman…whoever she was had so much time to take Destiny away from me while I was in purgatory without her.

Back in the condo I came to share with Destiny, I paced around the bed we shared as I tried to figure out what to do. After all we've shared, waiting so long to see me again was going to be hard on her too, I figured. It had to be. I knew Destiny only said those things because that wild haired woman was within earshot. That woman looked dangerous, and Destiny was probably doing what she needed to do to protect herself. Destiny told me not to write her again, but that was before my visiting restriction was put into place. She couldn't have meant that now. She would've understood why I had to write her.

I sat on our bed with a pen and notebook and wrote to Destiny. I told her how much I loved and missed her, vowed to stay faithful to her and keep faith that we would one day be together again. I apologized for my outburst and told her how our visit being cut short left me with no time to show her my new tattoo. I added her name to my right sleeve. I wanted to get her name across my heart, too, and promised to have it done in time for our next visit. I informed her that I understood she was trying to spare my feelings by not making me wait around for her, but not having any attachment to her in my life was more painful than I could bare.

Tearing the pages out of the notebook, I rushed to find an envelope and was back out the house to head to the post office.

Chapter 8

I was back at the prison ninety-one days later. I took the day off work just so I wouldn't have to wait the extra couple of days until my next day off to see Destiny. *My Destiny.*

I sat in the visiting room anxiously awaiting my love. My mind poured over all the letters I wrote her while I couldn't come up here to see her. Some days I wrote her twice a day. Needless to say, I became a regular at the post office, but I didn't get a single letter back from Destiny. I reminded myself to ask her if there was something wrong with her commissary because I put money on her books with every paycheck I received to make sure she had whatever she needed, including paper and pencil to write me back.

A guard came up to me. "You're waiting for Destiny Chambers?"

"Yes."

"She isn't coming."

"What do you mean? Is something wrong? Is she sick?" Panic rose in my chest. I had been away from her for too long and now something was wrong. It was something bad, I knew it. That would explain why she never wrote me back.

"Destiny is fine. She just doesn't want to see you," the guard informed me.

I paused for a few moments. "That has to be a mistake. Of course, she wants to see me. We…we have to see each other."

ADDICT 2.0 – ANDRE'S STORY

"Sorry pal. She told me to give this to you." He handed me a bundle of envelopes secured with thick rubber bands. My letters. Most of them weren't even opened.

It was the dick for me. I don't feel that way about you. You're obsessed.

Her words that I took as her trying to let me off the hook of waiting for her played back in my head. She wasn't letting me off the hook. Destiny meant them. She didn't want to see me while I spent every waking hour that I wasn't at work in our bed after spraying it with her perfume just to feel like she was close to me.

The entire time I had not been with another. Not even when she invited those damn twins in on what we had. I let her play out her fantasies and didn't complain even though it hurt me. I stood by her when no one else did. I loved her when no one else did.

I gathered the flowers I brought as well as the letters given back to me and walked to the exit and my car like a wounded dog. I've never been at such a loss. The woman I loved, the woman I gave up so much of myself for, didn't want to see me and she didn't love me back.

Protect yourself or she will hurt you. DeAngelo's words to me on the night we met played in my head. What I now realized, and he didn't, was that no hurt would have been had if he never came around. If he would have stayed away from Destiny, his brother would still be alive, and I would have had the time needed to make Destiny fall in love with me. We'd be in our home, in our bed, happy and satiated.

The wild haired woman turned Destiny from me, but she was only able to do that because those fucking twins took Destiny from me first. I couldn't get to the woman. At this point, she wasn't a factor. It was the twins. One of them was already dead from the pain he caused the woman I loved. Now it was time to make the other one pay.

DeAngelo had to die.

Porsha Deun

ADDICT 2.0 – ANDRE'S STORY

A Note from the Author:

Thank you for reading my book! I feel honored, truly. A special thank you to everyone who read and loved the first book of this series, Addict – A Fatal Attraction Story! This book (and the two coming behind it) exist because of you! I would have never poked and prodded at Andre, DeAngelo, and DeMario to tell me their stories if it were not for you, because in my mind, Addict was going to be a standalone book!

Oh, but a few of you would not leave me alone about it. I mean, y'all were really on my back and it worked out for the best! Now, that does not mean such tactics would work for future books. I am putting my foot down! Lol.

Andre, Andre, Andre. It was messy inside his head. Poor thing never stood a chance with Destiny. If he had fallen in love with any other woman, I would imagine that he would be insufferable. But his story isn't quite over yet. You see how things turn out for him in Addict 3.0 – DeAngelo's Story, which releases a few weeks after this book!

ADDICT 2.0 – ANDRE'S STORY

Did you enjoy Addict 2.0 – Andre's Story? Be sure to leave a review on Amazon, Goodreads, Bookbub, or my Facebook Page!

You can preview and purchase the rest of my books on my website, as well as with your favorite online book retailer! Be sure to sign up for my mailing list while you are on my website. My Love Bugs get cover reveals at least a month before the public, as well as surprises and giveaways.
www.porshadeun.com.

Love Lost Series
Love Lost
Love Lost Forever
Love Lost Revenge

Addict Series
Addict – A Fatal Attraction Story
Addict 2.0 – Andre's Story
Addict 3.0 – DeAngelo's Story (July 2021)
Addict 4.0 – DeMario's Story (August 2021)

Standalones
Intoxic (October 2021)

Children's Book
Princesses Can Do Anything!

Made in the USA
Columbia, SC
27 May 2021